ZACH KING

THE MAGICAL MIX-UP

BULLDOGS

Illustrated by

BEVERLY ARCE

THE
MAGICAL
MIX-UP

PUFFIN

PUFFIN BOOKS

UK | USA | Canada | Ireland | Australia
India | New Zealand | South Africa

Puffin Books is part of the Penguin Random House group of companies
whose addresses can be found at global.penguinrandomhouse.com.

www.penguin.co.uk
www.puffin.co.uk
www.ladybird.co.uk

First published in the United States of America by HarperCollins
Children's Books and in Great Britain by Puffin Books 2018

001

Text copyright © Zach King, 2018
Illustrations copyright © Beverly Arce, 2018

The moral right of the author and illustrator has been asserted

Set in 11.64/20.88 pt Sabon by Jouve (UK), Milton Keynes
Printed in Italy by LEGO SpA

A CIP catalogue record for this book is available from the British Library

ISBN: 978–0–241–32188–1

All correspondence to:
Puffin Books
Penguin Random House Children's
80 Strand, London WC2R 0RL

MIX
Paper from
responsible sources
FSC
www.fsc.org   FSC® C018179

Penguin Random House is committed to a
sustainable future for our business, our readers
and our planet. This book is made from Forest
Stewardship Council® certified paper.

A special thank-you to my incredible wife for letting me spend many late nights working on this book. To my fans around the world, I hope you enjoy this magical book!

Zach

ZACH'S KING-DOM

AARON
-loves Michael the Cat
-Is the official "Camera Guy"
-Is 12 years old
FANCY!
Cheese!!!
=AARON=
Why do all animals like u?
-Cuz I'm COOL!!!
lol, sure

Michael the cat
- Perfect in every way
- Afraid of heights
cute
Michael
AMAZING!
Marvelous!
WONDERFUL!
fantastic!
look! he signed
OMG. look @ his lil

RACHEL HOLM
- 11 years old
- loves the rodeo
- Used to live in Wyoming
- KARATE!!!
Nice!
Thank you!
Rachel
POW
"There's a
Snake in

to rule them all!
The Kings (zach's fam)
Mom has a magic ring
Dad has a magic watch
funny
DAD
Sophie
MOM
Sophie is Zach's little sister
Sophie has magic glasses

THE ADVENTURE BEGINS....

CHAPTER 1

"Go!" Rachel shouted. "I can't hold him much longer!"

She rode the giant alligator like a wild horse that had to be broken. Jawzilla, an enormous, slimy, scaly, mean-faced gator, had been magically transported into the principal's office from the zoo by Zach

King's magic snapbacks—and it was about to get loose. Three other kids, including Zach, scrambled to keep away from the gator's snapping jaws.

Zach knew what he had to do. Rachel couldn't hold Jawzilla forever. He grabbed his magical snapbacks, which operated like portals from one cap to the other, and tricked the gator into jumping into one cap. Then, Zach spun around and flushed the other cap down the toilet in the principal's private bathroom. The gator vanished down the toilet, which gurgled briefly and then exploded spectacularly, spraying water all over the trashed office. . . .

"Those were the days." Aaron sighed as he watched the alligator video on his phone for what must have been the hundredth time. "Man, I wish you still had your magic."

"Tell me about it," Zach agreed as the two boys walked across the parking lot toward the front entrance of the mall. He yanked his distracted friend out of the way of an oncoming car. "It's like I'm right back where I started—nowhere."

It had actually been only a few weeks since Zach's

magic snapbacks had been wrecked, but he was already tired of being an ordinary kid. Zach came from a whole family of modern-day magicians. All the Kings had a unique object that enabled them to use magic—and Zach was all too aware that to save his friends, he might have flushed his magic powers away forever.

Or had he?

The clear glass doors of the mall entrance tempted Zach. Once, not too long ago, he had somehow passed through a similar door like a ghost. Maybe he could still pull off that trick, even without his snapbacks?

It was worth a try.

"Get your phone camera ready," he told Aaron, who was all about capturing cool stuff on video. "I'm going for it!"

"Again?"

Zach had been trying to restart his magic for weeks without success, but this time would be different . . . just because. Taking a deep breath, he backed up to get a running start, then sprinted straight toward the closed door. In his head, he imagined himself passing through the solid glass as though it wasn't there.

I can do this, he thought. *I have to do this.*

WHAM!

His face collided with the door. Instead of passing through it, he bounced off it, stumbling backward into Aaron, who yelped in protest. Puzzled shoppers stopped to stare at Zach, who felt like a total dork. His nose didn't feel too great either.

"Ouch," he said, clutching his bruised beak.

Aaron checked his phone. "I'm guessing that's not what you wanted me to film."

"Not exactly." Zach sighed and shook his head. "I was sure I could do it again."

"There's got to be a trick to it. We just need to work together to figure it out," Aaron offered helpfully as the friends entered the mall and made their way to the food court. Zach's nose was still smarting as they settled into a booth at a diner-style fast food place and treated themselves to milk shakes and a big plate of fries.

The mall diner was one of Zach and Aaron's favorite spots. The fries were crispy, the burgers were cheap, no one rushed them out, and there was always a buzz of activity around.

Hungry shoppers streamed past them as Aaron couldn't

resist playing the alligator video again. Zach noted that the video, their most popular ever, had just rolled past fifty thousand views. He wondered how many of those were just from his friend watching it again and again and again.

"Seriously, dude, we gotta do something," Aaron insisted, nervously tugging on the collar of his shirt, like he was trying to escape from it. "No magic means no more cool YouTube videos, which means we're going to start losing subscribers quick, which means we're going to be yesterday's news. We have to find a way to get you your mojo back."

Aaron's videos of Zach's magic tricks had helped them both become a little more popular at school and online, so Zach couldn't blame his friend for wanting to keep the videos coming after being picked on for years. As for Zach, he was still new to public school, having been homeschooled for most of his life, and the online magic tricks had made fitting in a whole lot easier. Neither of the boys was exactly part of the in crowd these days, like Tricia, or considered as cool as Rachel, but they weren't at the bottom of the food chain anymore either.

"Magical objects just don't grow on trees, you know," Zach said. "Well, except for my uncle Elvis's object. He has a magical leaf. Dude gets super nervous every fall. It's not easy to find one lost leaf if it's been swept up in a huge pile. . . ."

"I'm serious," Aaron continued. "We can't start coasting on reruns. We need new content to protect our brand."

"Our brand?"

"Sure." Aaron explained, "we're the magic trick guys. We gotta keep doing bigger and more eye-popping magic tricks or our audience will go somewhere else."

"If you say so," Zach said.

To be honest, Zach was less worried about their "brand" than about Rachel, whom he'd had a crush on ever since the minute he'd met her. And it was his magic videos that had first gotten her attention. Would she still like him if he couldn't do magic anymore?

He glanced down at the clock on his phone. Rachel was supposed to have joined them by now. Was he just being paranoid, or was she late more and more often lately?

"I don't know what to tell you, man," he said to Aaron. "The snapbacks are gone. My magic is gone.

We're going to have rely on your cat, Michael, being cute to get views."

"Michael is on hiatus."

"Hiatus? How can a cat be on hiatus?"

"Creative differences." Aaron glanced around, then lowered his voice. "Between you and me, Michael has become a bit of a diva. He won't even purr for the camera without a bonus tuna treat." He let out a weary sigh. "Actors."

"Well, then, we're toast. You only get one magical item," Zach told his friend. "That's just how it works."

"But what if it isn't?" Aaron called up another video on his phone. "Watch this one again."

The video, which Aaron had recorded just days after the alligator incident, showed Zach suffering a serious brain freeze after sucking down an ice-cream soda too fast. He smacked one side of his head and ice cubes tumbled out of his ear, clattering onto the table. "See—magic!" Aaron pointed at the screen. "And you did that without the snapbacks."

"Yeah, maybe," Zach said. "But I have no idea how."

"That's what we have to figure out." Aaron shoved

a metal mixing cup full of ice-cold chocolate shake toward Zach.

"Seriously?" Zach protested. "But I'm stuffed!"

"It's science, dude. We have to keep experimenting until we figure it out."

"It's not science. It's magic. And seriously?"

"Seriously," Aaron said. He called the waitress over and asked her to bring one of every flavor shake they had.

"No way," Zach protested. "More brain freeze isn't going to prove anything."

"Well, then, you tell me how we're going to get your magic back," Aaron said. "What else did you have with you right before your head turned into an ice-cube maker?"

Zach searched his memory. "A Popsicle, I think. And before that, some fries with ketchup."

"Ketchup, you say?" Aaron's eyes lit up. "Just like the first time, the day we met, with the snack machine!"

Zach knew exactly what Aaron was talking about. On his very first day at Horace Greeley, Zach had fallen into a cafeteria snack machine, passing like a ghost through the clear glass front of the machine, and it'd happened right after being "ketchupped" by Tricia Stands and her mean-girl friends. He never had figured out how or why he'd pulled off that trick. Or why he'd never been able to duplicate it.

"What?" he asked. "You think the ketchup triggered the magic?"

"Why not?" Aaron said. "It seems like the common element both times you did magic without the snapbacks!"

Excited, Aaron reached across the table and grabbed the red plastic ketchup bottle.

"Wait! What are you—" Zach complained, but too late! Aaron pointed the bottle at Zach, squeezed hard, and squirted ketchup all over Zach's favorite hoodie.

"Is it working?" Aaron asked. "Do you feel anything?"

"Besides annoyed?" Zach tried to wipe off the ketchup with a napkin, but he just ended up smearing the bright-red goo all over the place. He looked like the victim in a slasher movie. The more he dabbed at it, the worse it got. "Have you lost your marbles?"

"Never mind that. Try the ice cube trick again," Aaron urged. "Let's see if the ketchup makes a difference!"

"I'm not hungry!"

"Just go with it."

"Okay, fine. Whatever."

Zach sucked down a big slurp of ice-cold ice cream shake as quickly as he could. The freeze went straight to his brain. He winced in pain.

Aaron held up his phone to record the results of the test. "Anything? Shake your head. Like you did last time."

Zach shook his head.

"Harder," Aaron urged.

He shook hard—but not a single ice cube tumbled out.

"Nothing." Zach shrugged. "Maybe I just had some leftover magic that one time."

"I don't know." Aaron looked reluctant to give up on his theory. He scratched his chin like a scientist pondering a difficult equation. "Perhaps we just need to find the right kind of ketchup . . . or maybe some mustard or mayonnaise?"

Zach groaned.

There *had* to be a better way to get his magic back!

CHAPTER 2

Zach came back from the bathroom with a huge, wet patch on his hoodie. He'd done his best to wipe off the ketchup, but it'd been impossible to get it completely clean with just hot water and hand soap. He settled back into the booth across from Aaron and noticed that all the shakes his friend had ordered had arrived. And that Aaron actually had done a pretty good job finishing off a few on his own.

"Hey, you going to the school dance on Friday?" Zach asked as casually as he could.

"I suppose," Aaron said. "Wanna go over together?"

"Well, actually, I'm thinking of inviting Rachel."

Aaron put down his phone. "Rachel? Well, you better hurry. She's a superstar now, thanks to our alligator-wrestling video, which everybody at school has seen." Aaron was understandably proud of capturing Rachel's exploits on camera while the rest of them were just trying to avoid being gobbled. "Heck, she's even running for class president now."

"I know," Zach said. "That's why I have to wow her with the coolest invite ever. . . . I'm thinking about delivering the invitation by *drone*."

"Do you even have a drone?" Aaron asked.

"Well, not exactly."

"And if you got one, you sure you could pilot it?"

"Not exactly."

"And you're still completely out of magic, right?"

"That's not the point," Zach complained. "The point is to wow her, and dropping in with a drone-powered invite—she can't say no to that."

"True dat," Aaron said, offering Zach a fist bump. "So how—"

Aaron shut up abruptly—mostly because Zach had reached across the table and clamped a hand over his mouth.

"Hey, Zach," Rachel called from across the restaurant. "Hey, Aaron."

"Hey," Zach said back.

"Mmrrph," Aaron said, since Zach's hand was still over his mouth.

Every time Zach saw Rachel, it was like the first time again. Zach was convinced that she was the prettiest girl he'd ever seen. Her long, brown hair and amazing brown eyes took his breath away. Today, she was dressed super casually—a T-shirt, jeans, and cowboy boots. Fashion was the least of her interests, but she somehow always managed to look a hundred times better than all the girls wearing the latest designer duds.

"Sssh!" Zach whispered to Aaron. "Not a word about the dance or the drone to Rachel. I want to surprise her."

"Mrow wips wre swerealed," he said.

"What?" Zach asked, and Aaron lowered his glance toward Zach's hand still clamped over his mouth. "Oh, sorry."

"My lips are sealed."

Rachel waved to the boys again as she headed over to say hi, but before she got to their table, a younger kid, who looked like he was nine or so, rushed toward her.

"You're her, aren't you?" he exclaimed. "The girl who wrestled that alligator in the video? That was just savage . . . and brave! I've watched that video a zillion times already, and so have all my friends!"

"It's not a zillion," Aaron whispered to Zach. "We only have 50,201 total views."

"Thanks," Rachel told the kid. "It was no big deal. I grew up on a farm. To me, that gator was just another critter to wrangle."

Like Zach, Rachel was new to Horace Greeley Middle School. Her family had only recently moved to the area from Wyoming.

The star-struck kid held out a napkin and a felt-tip pen. "Could . . . could I have your autograph?"

"You bet." Rachel gave Zach and Aaron an apologetic look as she graciously took the time to sign the napkin. Grinning from ear to ear, the kid wandered away to show off the autograph to his parents, who seemed utterly dumbfounded, and Rachel headed toward Zach and Aaron. "Sorry I'm late, guys. Hope I didn't keep you waiting."

"Nope," Zach lied. "I know you're busy these days."

"You have no idea," she sighed. "Who knew running for class president would be so time-consuming? But I have tons of exciting ideas for our school, like adding class-grown fruits and vegetables to the lunch menu, or maybe starting a local 4-H club, which could make Horace Greeley an even cooler and healthier place to get a good education." She nodded at Aaron. "Thanks for the cool campaign video, BTW. It looks great!"

Aaron grinned, proud of his work. "Nothing but the best for Team Rachel."

"Not a bad campaign slogan," she joked. "Although maybe we should it flip it around to say that our school deserves the best."

"Well, you can count on my vote," Zach said. "I can't think of anyone better for the job."

"And anyone would be better than Tricia Stands," Aaron added. "No offense."

"None taken," Rachel said. "I know exactly what you mean."

Tricia was their school's Number One Mean Girl. A bully in designer skirts, she had been making Aaron's life miserable for years. Her power and popularity had taken a tumble

after the Jawzilla video—since Zach, Rachel, and Aaron had swooped in to rescue her. But Tricia wasn't one to give up being top dog for long. Her path to getting back to being the most popular kid in school was all based on her being the next class president.

"I want to represent our entire class, make the school better for everyone," Rachel continued. "Tricia is just going to look out for what she likes and for her own clique of 'popular' kids . . . and ignore everybody else."

"Like my new AV Club?" Aaron asked.

Riding the popularity of Zach's YouTube videos, Aaron had launched the AV Club to help other kids learn to make awesome online videos. It immediately became one of the most popular after-school activities, and so, of course, Tricia Stands hated it.

"Yep," Rachel said. "The AV Club, the Robotics Club, the Cosplay Club, the Steampunk Alliance, my proposed 4-H club—they're all toast if Tricia gets control of the class budget. Unless you're into sports or fashion, you're out of luck."

"Well, the good news is that she doesn't stand a chance against you," Zach said. "You're a lock."

"Well, I hope you're right, but I don't take anything for granted with Tricia around."

Zach felt the same way. "Well, don't forget your other competition," he joked to lighten the mood. "Horace the bulldog."

Horace was the school's mascot: a pudgy American bulldog who spent most of his day snoring (and drooling) in his bed by the trophy case. As a gag, he was officially running for class president too.

"Right," Rachel said, playing along. "That's the candidate I *really* need to worry about."

She was about to slide into the booth beside Zach when a booming voice suddenly called out from right behind him.

"Hey, Rachel! Looking good!"

Zach turned around in surprise to see another boy,

about their age, sitting in the booth behind theirs.

"Oh, hey, Hogan!" Rachel replied warmly. "I didn't see you there at first." She turned toward Zach and Aaron. "Have you guys met Hogan yet? His family just moved here from Australia—can you believe it?"

"G'day, mates." Hogan rose to greet Rachel. He was tall and tanned, with long hair, blue eyes, and a cool cowboy-style hat. An Aussie accent advertised his roots. He grinned at Zach and Aaron. "Nice to meet you, mates."

"Um, hi," Zach said, wanting to be friendly. He had seen Hogan around school but hadn't really met him yet. "Welcome to the USA."

How long was he sitting behind us? Zach wondered. *And how much did he overhear?*

"You guys should get to know Hogan," Rachel said, a little more enthusiastically than Zach would have liked. "He grew up in the outback and can break a wild stallion, lasso and tie a hog in less than seven seconds, box a kangaroo, and do all sorts of awesome stuff!"

"Says the champion alligator wrassler in these parts," Hogan said, flashing a brilliant white smile. "You sure

you're not actually from Down Under?" he teased her.

"Nope, I'm one-hundred-percent All-American," she said proudly. "We grow 'em tough here too, you know."

"Fair dinkum," he said, grinning.

Zach guessed that was Aussie for "true enough" or "for sure" or something like that.

"Shake?" Aaron offered. He'd drunk four of the five milk shakes he'd ordered and was looking, frankly, a bit green. "I don't think I can finish another."

"These your friends?" Hogan asked.

"Sure are," Rachel said proudly.

"Well, any friends of yours are friends of mine," he said, giving Zach a stiff handshake and Aaron a hard pat on the back. Zach was afraid it was enough to dislodge whatever Aaron couldn't quite digest. But Aaron seemed to swallow back down whatever was trying to come up. "Your friend Rachel here is quite the all-arounder. Wrestling gators, doing karate, running for class president—that's what I call a real can-do attitude. Like we say Down Under, go big or go home."

Aaron raised an eyebrow. "Er, I don't think that's a specifically Australian saying."

"Pretty sure it is, mate," Hogan said confidently. "Anyway, I gotta run. See you all around school." He smirked at Rachel. "Especially you, Gator Girl."

"Absolutely," Rachel replied. "See ya, Hogan."

Zach wanted to barf. When did Rachel and Hogan get to be such good buddies anyway?

Something about the cocky Australian kid rubbed Zach the wrong way, but Hogan was new at school, just like Zach had been not too long ago, so Zach figured he owed him the benefit of the doubt.

He reached over and grabbed that last milk shake from Aaron and took a big, healthy sip of it. And while Zach's mouth was full of strawberry milk shake, Aaron leaned over and whispered to Zach, "If I were you, I'd get going with that drone—ASAP."

CHAPTER 3

"Who wants cake?" Mrs. King asked before dumping a heap of flour, sugar, and raw eggs on the kitchen island countertop. She twisted the crystal ring on her right hand—just a quick back-and-forth, like she was adjusting the temperature in the bath—and abracadabra! A triple-decker birthday cake, complete with rich chocolate frosting, appeared. It smelled fresh out of the oven, and Zach's mouth watered in anticipation.

"Now all we need are a hundred and seventeen candles," she said.

The entire King clan, a small army of uncles, aunts, and cousins, had convened at Great-Grandpa King's cabin for his 117th birthday. Great-Grandpa King's cabin was hidden away high in the mountains, overlooking a sparkling lake. It was remote enough to guarantee plenty of privacy. And Great-Grandpa King needed his privacy. He was probably the most powerful magician of the whole family, which was saying something. Magic ran in the King family. Except for Zach, everyone at the party had their own unique power, but among them only Great-Grandpa King was immortal. Well, not so much strictly immortal as just that he had the ability to be however old he wanted to be. So even though he'd been alive for 117 years, he looked like a teenager. His magical object was a special fountain pen, and every year after he blew out the candles for another birthday, he just wrote down the age he wanted to be, and—presto, change-o—that's how old he was. It really was amazing, but then Zach's whole family was pretty amazing. Well, everyone, that is, except Zach. Without his snapbacks, Zach was the only King in generations not to have powers. But he tried not to let that bother him as he watched his relatives do their things.

"Hi, everybody!" Gwen popped up on the computer screen to join the party in virtual reality. "Looks like I streamed in just in time for dessert."

Gwen reached out through the screen to grab two plates of cake off the counter. "Your mom outdid herself this year," she said, handing Zach the smaller of the two pieces. "If I had her power, I'd weigh seven hundred pounds. Remember that party where she made giant fried turkey legs for everyone? OMG—so delicious."

"Yep. That was the same year that she made that chocolate fondue fountain," Zach added, shaking his head. "I had a stomachache for days after that."

The cousins laughed at the memory, and Zach was secretly happy that Gwen hadn't brought up the last family party, when Zach had tried to steal the family talent show by attempting to fly using a couple dozen super-shaken soda bottles. Mom had been forced to use her powers to turn a tablecloth into an enormous pillow to soften Zach's crash landing so he wouldn't break his skull.

"Can I ask you for a favor?" Zach had been waiting all afternoon for Gwen to log on so he could ask for her help, but now that she was on the screen in front of him, he found himself tongue-tied. "Next week there's, like, this big dance at school. . . . And there's this girl. . . . And I really want to impress her. . . . And I had this idea . . ."

"Just spit it out, cuz. What do you need?"

"Can you download a drone for me?"

"Is that all? No problem. The way you were talking, I thought you wanted me to download her." She tapped quickly on her keyboard and called up a photo of a drone from a home shopping site. Zach's cousin Benny came in just as she slid the image off the screen into real life. Benny caught the full-size gadget and handed it to Zach. The remote-controlled quadcopter weighed several ounces and felt perfectly solid. In theory, it had more than enough lifting power to deliver a dance invitation to a certain well-known cowgirl. "Drones are easy. People are hard. You know what happened the last time I tried to flick a person off the screen?"

"Do I want to know?" Zach asked.

"The thing is, conjured items don't last long. They fade away after a few days. Fine for an inanimate thing. Not

so cool when a live person suddenly starts to fade away."

"Seriously?"

"Yeah. Never again. It's just too freaky when someone starts to pixelate right in front of you. Oh, don't worry," she said, noticing Zach's gape-mouthed distress, "he was fine. He just went back to where he'd been—a little disoriented, maybe, and just in his boxer shorts, but good as new."

"So how long do I have with it?" Zach asked, holding up the drone.

"Hard to say exactly—but figure about twenty-four hours."

"Perfect," Zach said. He'd ask Rachel to the dance tomorrow, right before school. "You're a lifesaver."

She shrugged. "What else is family for?" She glanced down at her empty plate. "Let's see if there's any cake left."

"You want this piece?" a new voice piped up. "I'm not going to finish it anyway."

Zach's little sister, Sophie, appeared out of nowhere, holding a barely touched slice of cake. Her hot-pink glasses gave her the power to turn invisible at will. Zach never really knew whether she was around or not. He sometimes thought that this was just about the worst possible power a little sister could have.

"Sophie!" he blurted. "How long have you been here?"

"Long enough." She was two years younger than Zach, and barely half his height, but she often acted as though she was the older sibling instead. "Nice drone, bro. Let me guess. This has something to do with Rachel?"

"Rachel, eh? Is that the girl you're going to ask to the dance?" Gwen asked.

Zach blushed in embarrassment.

"You're asking Rachel to the dance?" Sophie yelped. "Way to go, big bro."

"You think he has a chance?" Gwen asked.

"If he plays it cool," Sophie told her cousin.

"So, none at all," Gwen cracked. The two girls laughed. Zach took the teasing in the way it was meant. He knew they both loved him and would always have his back, but still, that they doubted him just made him all the more determined to wow Rachel and take her to the dance.

CHAPTER 4

On Monday morning, Zach woke early to make sure he got to school before Rachel did. He was waiting on the sidewalk in front of the main entrance when her school bus pulled up. The drone hovered out of sight, ready to deliver a handwritten invitation to the dance. Zach had spent hours writing and rewriting it until the note was just right: friendly but not too mushy, casual

but not too casual, funny but not too jokey. He'd triple-checked the spelling, too.

"Make sure you stay in frame," Aaron yelled over to Zach.

Aaron was on hand to film the Big Moment. Zach flashed his friend a thumbs-up, but honestly, he wasn't sure he really wanted the moment up on social media. But Aaron had insisted. Subscriber numbers were slowing down. They needed something fresh, and Aaron was convinced that this would be it. "Perfect," Aaron yelled back after Zach shimmied over a step. "Scene one, take one: Ask Rachel to the Dance. Ready when you are," Aaron said, utterly unconcerned about who else could overhear.

Zach gulped and glanced down at his phone, which had the drone-control app open. His hands were sweaty. His stomach churned. He held the device tightly, as if it might decide to run away at the last moment. Zach was way too aware of just how many other kids were milling around in front of the school. One way or another, he was going to have an audience.

He gulped again as Rachel's bus pulled up and she stepped out onto the sidewalk.

This is it, he thought.

Rachel gaped at Hogan in surprise, caught completely off-guard by both the drone and the invitation. She wasn't sure what to say. Stalling, she nodded at the campaign button on his shirt.

"Nice button," she said. "Does this mean I've got your vote?"

"Count on it." He flashed a gleaming smile at her. "I can't think of anyone else I'd rather vote for . . . or take to the dance."

"Good answer," she admitted. "Both parts."

"So what do you say?" Hogan asked as his drone hovered overhead. It whirred faintly in the background. "Shall we give it a whirl?"

Rachel hesitated, awkwardly shifting the bouquet from one arm to the other. To be honest, she had been hoping that Zach would ask her to the dance, but if he wasn't going to get around to it . . .

Plus, she thought, *that* was *a pretty neat trick with the drone.*

"Sure," she said. "Why not? Sounds like fun."

"Aces!" he twanged. "Can't wait!"

She glanced over at Zach, who was hanging out with

Aaron as usual. They were eyeballing the drone like everyone else.

Sorry, Zach, she thought. *You snooze, you lose.*

"You're not going to let him get away with this, are you?" Aaron asked Zach, sounding indignant on his friend's behalf. "Stealing your idea, I mean."

Zach stared bleakly at the control app on his phone. His own drone was still ready to go, but what was the point? Hogan had beaten him to the punch, big-time.

"What can I do?" Zach said. "It's not fair, but . . ."

Principal Riggs stormed onto the scene, scowling. He was a stocky older man wearing a wool sweater. A bushy mustache and goatee made up for the lack of hair on his head. "What's all this commotion?"

The principal was only a year away from retiring and moving to Florida to take up fishing full-time. (Zach had spent enough time in his office that he couldn't have helped but notice all the vacation brochures and fishing-boat catalogs that the principal had lying around.) And so now more than ever, Principal Riggs had a zero-tolerance policy when it came to any kind of surprises and shenanigans. He wanted a quiet last year before he sailed off into the sunset, and Zach was sure a drone delivery interrupting the beginning of a school day was exactly the sort of thing that would make the grumpy principal blow his top.

Zach *almost* felt sorry for Hogan.

"G'day, mate!" Hogan greeted the principal confidently. He didn't look at all worried about getting into trouble. "How'd those fly lures I lent you work out? Catch anything? Those tips I gave you help at all?"

"Caught my limit!" Riggs bragged, momentarily distracted. Then he noticed the drone hovering overhead and got back to business. "Hogan?" He glanced around, taking in the situation. "Are you responsible for this . . . hoopla?"

"You bet," Hogan said. "Is there a problem?"

The principal hesitated. "Well, ordinarily, we frown on such disturbances, but you're new here, so I suppose you can be forgiven for not yet being fully aware of our rules." He raised his voice to be heard by the other students. "But don't the rest of you start getting any ideas. There'll be no more unauthorized aircraft on

or above this campus, not while I'm principal—which won't be too much longer, thank goodness!"

"Thanks, mate," Hogan said. "I didn't mean to cause any fuss."

"I know you didn't." The principal slapped Hogan on the back as he cast a disparaging glance at Zach and Aaron. "Some of you troublemakers could learn a thing or two from his sterling example."

Zach couldn't believe his ears.

"He's got them all fooled," Zach said. "He's up to something. He's got to be."

"Well, he ruined our video, if that's what you mean. This was about the most boring film since *Mars Needs Moms*," Aaron said as he clicked off his video camera.

"He's not going to get away with it—whatever it is," Zach said, pounding his fist into his hand. "Not if Zach King has anything to say about it!" But Aaron didn't hear him. He was completely focused on the drone that was becoming pixelated as it fell out of the sky.

"Um, Zach," Aaron said, pointing up, but too late. Zach fumbled for the controls, but not before someone yelled, "Look out!" Principal Riggs spun around, saw the drone heading straight for him, jumped out of the way, tripped, and spilled coffee all over himself. Inches before the drone was about to smash into him, it magically disappeared—just as Gwen had predicted.

"Zach King!" Principal Riggs yelled. But Zach didn't care about that. He was more worried about the fact that nobody—including Rachel—realized that Hogan was the sort of no-good skunk who would steal another guy's idea and take credit for it.

"I need to warn her," he told Aaron.

"Warn who?"

"Rachel. This Hogan fellow can't be trusted."

"*Zach!*" Principal Riggs yelled again. "My office—now!"

"How does he know it was your drone?" Aaron asked, but Zach just shrugged. He had bigger things to worry about.

CHAPTER 5

"Hey, Rachel, can we talk?"

She was putting the fresh bouquet of flowers away in her locker when Zach came up to her between classes.

"Sure. What's up?" she asked as she closed her locker door.

"I just . . ." Zach kicked the ground. He wasn't sure what he wanted to say. He knew that he had to warn Rachel about what Hogan was really like. "I just thought you should know that Hogan stole that drone idea from me. The whole stunt with the drone delivering an invite to the dance. That was *my* idea. Hogan eavesdropped on me at the mall the other day."

Rachel frowned. "Hang on. You were also planning to ask me to the dance?"

"Maybe," Zach admitted. He couldn't tell from her tone what she thought about that. "But that doesn't matter now."

"And why not?" Rachel asked, folding her arms over her chest.

"Because you can't trust Hogan!" Zach said, raising his voice. He didn't want Rachel to think that he was just jealous because Hogan asked her first. Other kids had stopped heading to class to watch. With Zach King, you never knew what kind of show you were about to witness. "I know he must have some sneaky reason for inviting you."

"Because he couldn't possibly just want to go to the dance with *me*?" she said.

All the kids around her *oohed*. One even said, "Ouch, burn."

"No! I mean, yes, sort of, but not like that," he stammered. "I mean . . . this isn't coming out right at all."

"Sounds to me like maybe that drone of yours isn't the only thing that you've lost. I think you've lost your mind, too, Zach King. I'm sorry if you're disappointed about the dance, but Hogan really is a nice guy, and he asked me first. And you know what, the way you're acting now, I'm not sure I would say yes even if you had asked me first."

Zach hoped she didn't mean that. "He's got you fooled, Rachel—just like everyone else!"

"So now I'm a fool?"

"I'm just trying to protect you!" he insisted.

"From what, exactly?" she asked.

"Er, I'm still a little fuzzy on that part."

"Uh-huh," she said skeptically. "Well, let me know when you've got that worked out. In the meantime, I have to get to class." She pushed passed Zach, and the crowd parted as she left. She had wrestled an alligator. No one was getting in her way.

"But," Zach yelled after her, "you have to believe me. Hogan's no good!"

Rachel didn't want to hear any more of this. "See you later, Zach," she promised. "When you're acting more like yourself."

Zach kicked the locker hard enough to hard to hurt his toe. "Yowch," he yelped. "Stupid lockers."

"And cut," Aaron said. Zach hadn't even noticed him filming the whole thing. "Now that's what I call a compelling video. Much better. Thanks, Zach!"

Could this day get any worse?

CHAPTER 6

Now what to do? Zach wondered.

Zach's parents took him and Sophie to the mall after school. They had some boring errands to run. Something about a new rug and a replacement filter for Dad's fish tank. They gave Zach and Sophie ten dollars each and asked them to stay out of trouble for a half hour, please. Zach was only half listening, though. He was desperate to figure out what his next move was. There had to be some way to let Rachel know that Hogan wasn't really all that—without sounding like a sore loser.

And then it hit him: *I need to find out what Hogan really is up to.*

While Zach thought about *how* he'd figure that out, Sophie led the way toward the food court. The mall had just about every kind of fast food you could imagine, from pizza to burgers to Chinese food to juice bars and ice cream and something called "Dinner You Can Drink," which were health shakes that Zach suspected were little more than yogurt smoothies with wheat grass blended in. At the center of the seating area was a giant bubbling wishing fountain where people tossed loose change.

Sophie licked her lips. "You up for a milk shake?"

"No!" Zach said too emphatically. "I mean, I think I'm in the mood for something else today."

Sophie shrugged. "You sure? It's free supersize day."

"Nah." Zach came down the escalator to the food court. "I'm just not that—" he began when he spotted Rachel and Hogan sitting on a bench. They looked like they were having a good time together.

"Hide me," Zach said, ducking behind his sister.

"What? Why?" Sophie asked. "What's wrong?"

What if Rachel spotted him and invited them to join them? What if Hogan spotted him and had heard what Zach had been saying about him? What if they both saw him and thought he was stalking them? He wasn't ready to deal with any of that right here, right now, and on an empty stomach.

"Quick!" Zach said to Sophie. "Give me your hat and glasses!" For whatever reason, Sophie had left the house in a big floppy sun hat.

"Seriously?" She gave him a puzzled look. "What for?"

"I need a disguise," he said, "so Rachel over there doesn't see me. It works for Clark Kent."

"Fine. Whatever." Sophie handed him her hat and hot-pink glasses. "But you owe me a full explanation later."

"Sure, sure." Zach hastily put on the outfit. It wasn't a perfect fit, but he hoped it would be enough to make him incognito for a minute. He squinted through the prescription lenses. "How do they look? Do you think they'll recognize me?"

"OMG!" Sophie stared at him in shock. "Recognize you? They won't even be able to see you. Where did you go?"

"Huh?"

Sophie poked him in the chest—hard. "You're still here."

"Ow," Zach complained, rubbing his sternum. "That hurt."

"You're *invisible*, Zach! I can't see you, like, at all."

Zach glanced down—and he couldn't believe his eyes. He didn't see himself. No feet, no legs, no torso . . . nothing. He held up his hand before his face but saw only empty air where he felt his hand was. He wiggled invisible fingers.

"This is impossible!" Sophie said.

"No," Zach said, "this is *awesome*."

"But Zach, my glasses shouldn't work on you. You know that."

The way it went was that each person's magical object only worked for them. Only Sophie could use her glasses to turn invisible, just like only their mother could use her magic ring, or only Cousin Gwen could use her magic thumb drive, and so on, at least according to the rules. As far as the two kids knew, no King had ever been able to use another person's magical object in the entire history of magic. That Sophie's glasses had turned Zach invisible was just not supposed to happen.

"This is freaking amazing," Zach exclaimed.

"Keep your voice down." Sophie looked around to see if anyone had noticed Zach disappearing. "You want people to think the mall is haunted?"

"Right, right," Zach whispered. "Okay, I have to try this out. This is so cool. I definitely don't need to wear your hat anymore. I don't see why you don't just go invisible all the time."

"Careful, big brother. It's trickier to be invisible than it seems. It took me years of practice to master it, remember?"

Zach knew as well as anyone that mastering your magical powers takes practice. Before he started at Horace Greeley Middle School, he was homeschooled just like all the kids in the greater King family. It took years of training to learn to control your powers—and trying and failing had to be done at home to keep the King family's secret a secret. Zach was the exception to the rule. He went to regular school because his parents thought he'd been "skipped." They figured it would be best for him to get used to being normal since he seemingly had no powers of his own.

Unless, of course, he did.

"Sure, sure—be careful. No worries." Zach was eager to try out the magic glasses. "I've got this!"

"Famous last words," Sophie muttered.

Zach was tempted to eavesdrop on Rachel and Hogan, but when he turned to see what they were doing, he noticed that Rachel was getting up and saying good-bye to Hogan. He gulped as she spied Sophie and headed over, then remembered that Rachel couldn't see him. He slumped down out of sight anyway and tried not to make a sound.

Sure enough, Rachel paused as she walked by their bench.

"Oh, hi, Sophie," she said. "I almost didn't recognize you without your glasses." She glanced around. "Is Zach here?"

"I haven't seen him," Sophie said, smirking at her joke.

"Okay," Rachel said. Zach couldn't tell if she was disappointed or relieved that he was nowhere to be seen. "Tell him I said hi."

"Absolutely."

For a second, Zach was afraid that Rachel might actually bump into him, but then she continued on her way, exiting the food court. Sophie waited until Rachel was completely out of sight—in the ordinary way—before holding out her hand to Zach's apparently empty seat.

"She's gone. You can give me my glasses back."

"Not so fast," he whispered. "I've never been invisible before. I want to enjoy this a little more."

"Not a good idea, bro. Hand them over."

Ignoring her, Zach glanced over at Hogan. He was considering playing a prank on Hogan, just to get even for him stealing the drone idea, when, to his surprise, Tricia Stands—of all people—joined Hogan on the bench.

Whoa, Zach thought, *what are those two doing together?*

Tricia was blond, stylish, and spoiled rotten. Her designer clothes were trendy to the max, costing more than most people's laptops. Her last attempt to bully Zach and his friends had backfired on her badly by almost turning her into alligator chow. As far as Zach knew, she was still holding a grudge about that—and Zach knew she had to *hate* that Rachel was more popular than her now.

So what was Hogan doing talking to Tricia? That Hogan and Tricia even knew each other came as a surprise to Zach, but as far as he was concerned, seeing them together was like spotting two comic-book supervillains in the same place. Whatever they were up to couldn't be good for Rachel.

"My glasses?" Sophie asked again.

"Hold on," Zach said. "I need to hear what Hogan and Tricia are saying."

Looked like he had turned invisible just in time!

"Wait!" Sophie said. "You haven't had any practice at this."

"It's just invisibility. How hard can it be?"

Zach thought he was going to die of embarrassment. Blushing furiously, it took him a moment to remember that all he had to do was take off Sophie's glasses to make his invisible clothes reappear. He yanked off the glasses, becoming fully visible once more, but that still left him standing in a fountain.

Not a good look, he realized.

Confused, the security guard eyed Zach suspiciously. The uniformed rent-a-cop looked like he took his job very seriously. "Just what the heck is going on here?"

"Um, a ghost pushed me into the fountain?" Zach said, thinking fast. "Excuse me—I have to go check on my little sister!"

The bewildered guard was still scratching his head as Zach scrambled away to rejoin Sophie—and Rachel, who was staring at him in surprise. He couldn't quite read her expression. Was she embarrassed for him . . . or by him?

"Um, hi, Rachel," he said awkwardly. He wiped his wet hair away from his eyes. "What's new?"

She spotted Sophie's glasses in his hand and put two and two together. "Hang on, you were using Sophie's glasses to turn invisible?"

"Keep it down, please," Sophie cautioned as she took back her glasses. "But, yes, he was *trying* to use my powers . . . just not very well."

"Yeah, what happened there?" Zach asked. "What was I doing wrong?"

"Besides using my glasses without any practice?" Sophie sighed wearily. "It's like if the first time you ever rode a bike, you got on a ten-speed and tried to ride straight downhill—without any training wheels."

"But how was he able to use them at all?" Rachel asked. "I thought it was one customer per magic object."

"That's how it's supposed to work," Zach said, "but then I saw you and Hogan together—"

"Whoa there! You were spying on me and Hogan?" A shocked expression came over her face. "While you were invisible?"

"No!" Zach realized that he'd accidentally put his foot in his mouth again. "I was spying on Hogan and *Tricia*!" He tried frantically to explain so she wouldn't get the wrong idea. "They're plotting against you. They've got some sort of sneaky plan involving the dance. I heard them with my own ears . . . right before things kinda got out of control."

"And you ended up standing in the fountain in your underwear," Rachel said. She sounded distinctly unimpressed by Zach's story.

"Well, technically, I still had my clothes on. They were just invisible. But that's not the point," Zach insisted. "You can't trust Hogan."

Rachel looked around. "So where are Hogan and Tricia now?"

"They split a few minutes ago—right before you showed up!"

Even as he said it, Zach realized just how lame that sounded.

"I'm not making this up," he promised. "They were there, and I was invisible, but then they weren't and I wasn't!"

Rachel held up her hand to silence him.

"Stop it, Zach. I don't want to hear any more of this." She sounded more disappointed than angry. "Using magic to spy on Hogan. . . . He's the new kid. Just like we both were not so long ago. So don't go making it any harder on him than it has to be. That's not cool." She shook her head sadly. "You're better than this, Zach."

She spun around and stormed off without another word, leaving Zach and Sophie behind in the food court. Soaking wet and feeling like an idiot, Zach glumly watched Rachel go.

"Well, that went well," Sophie said.

CHAPTER 7

The theme of the dance was Country-Western Hoedown, so the gym's parquet floors were closed over the built-in swimming pool and the field house had been transformed into a make-believe ranch, complete with decorative haystacks, horseshoes, and life-size papier-mâché horses. The horses, which were positioned all around the gym, had been arts-and-crafts projects at school and were painted in a variety of colors, some more realistic than others. A mechanical bull rested atop some padded wrestling mats. Brightly colored balloons and fancy, shimmery streamers hung from the ceiling. The refreshment table held chips and veggies with *ranch* dip (get it?) and salsa, plus a large plastic punch bowl filled with fresh lemonade. A painted barn scene, borrowed from the Drama Club, hung on one wall. Rodeo scenes decorated the paper plates and cups. Even the school mascot had been given a farm-style makeover—a pair of plush cattle horns was strapped to Horace's head, making him look more like a miniature bull than a bulldog as he snoozed on a cozy bed of straw. A campaign poster over his head read:

Zach wondered who was responsible for the cowboy theme—Hogan, Rachel, Principal Riggs, or even Tricia? He wouldn't put it past Tricia to devise a plan to have Hogan show Rachel up on her own turf, as it were. Even Rachel had said that Hogan was pretty good at roping calves.

"Just our luck," Zach grumbled to Aaron. Zach had dressed in a clip-on tie and button-down shirt along with his best jeans and sneakers. "It's like the dance was deliberately designed to make Hogan look good."

"You're not wrong," his friend agreed. "That guy's not wasting any time when it comes to taking over."

Sure enough, Hogan was already taking advantage of the western theme to show off some fancy rope tricks. Wearing a fringed snakeskin jacket, he was twirling a lasso in the air, while a crowd of students and chaperones, including Rachel, *oohed* and *aahed* in appreciation. Even Principal Riggs was clapping enthusiastically—and Principal Riggs never clapped for anything! Zach barely recognized the principal with a smile on his face.

Zach had to admit that Hogan's trick roping was

impressive. He twirled the spinning lariat around his body and jumped back and forth through the loops while keeping the rope in motion. He did flat loops, vertical loops, even butterfly loops. It was a live-action rodeo show. Zach probably would have clapped himself if he hadn't known that, deep down inside, Hogan was just as snakelike as his shiny, scaly jacket.

The boys made their way around the gym, scoping out the scene before winding up by the refreshment table. Aaron had brought his cat, Michael, as his "date." The fluffy gray feline rested comfortably in a customized baby sling while Aaron live-streamed the dance with his camera. Michael waved his paws in time to the music. Zach sometimes wondered if that cat wasn't almost half human.

"So I guess you worked out your creative differences?" Zach said. "Or is Michael still on hiatus?"

Aaron shrugged. "We're in negotiations regarding the tuna issue."

"Well, just keep your eyes open," Zach said grimly. "We're here to help Rachel, remember?"

"You bet," Aaron said, as Michael mewed in agreement. "But what exactly are we here to help her with again?"

"I wish I knew," Zach admitted. "We just have to be ready and hope we can spring into action in time to save her from whatever Hogan and Tricia have up their sneaky sleeves."

"And to catch it all on video," Aaron said.

"Yeah. That, too."

Zach turned away to watch the scene and to try to act cool. But a second later, something cold and gooshie splashed against the back of Zach's neck. He spun around to see Aaron loading up a plastic spoon filled with ranch-flavored dip.

"Hey!" Zach blurted. "Did you just fling some dip at me?"

"Well, I figured if the ketchup didn't work, maybe other condiments would." He eyed Zach curiously. "So, you feeling the magic again?"

"No!" Zach took his jacket off and dabbed at the back of his neck. "All I'm feeling is cold dip under my collar!"

Michael mewed in Aaron's defense.

"If you want, Michael can lick that off for you," Aaron suggested helpfully. "Might make for a cute video, especially if you're ticklish."

"No thanks!"

A live band, the Buckeye Barn Razors, played country-rock music, luring the kids out onto the dance floor for some spirited line dancing. Zach tossed his jacket in the coat closet, and then he and Aaron chilled by the refreshments, not daring to leave their vantage point. Zach had a clear view of Hogan and Rachel, who seemed to be enjoying dancing together. Zach couldn't help noticing that she was looking prettier than ever. She was wearing a fashionable new dress along with her usual cowboy boots. Zach kicked himself again for not asking her when he'd had the chance. That should have been him dancing with her.

He had tried to warn her about Hogan again when they had first arrived at the dance, but she had shut him down before he'd gotten more than a few words out. "Not one word, Zach King," she'd said, obviously still upset with him. "Don't even think about trying to spoil tonight for me. I just want to have a good time—got that?"

Zach cringed at the memory as he spotted Tricia dancing nearby. She was wearing a rhinestone-studded dress, and her glittery cowboy hat was more sparkly than a tiara. She was with one of her favorite stooges, a beefy lunkhead named Lenny, who Tricia often enlisted when she needed help carrying out her mean schemes.

But Zach wasn't going to let Tricia prank Rachel tonight, no matter what she and Hogan might have planned.

Not on my watch, Zach vowed, downing a cup of lemonade in one gulp. *No, not on my watch.*

Rachel spotted Zach and Aaron (and Michael) over by the refreshments. She was kind of surprised that either of them had showed up for the dance, since it wasn't really Aaron's thing, and as for Zach . . . well, she hoped he wasn't going to make a scene. With Hogan.

I can look out for myself, she thought, *thank you very much.*

So far the only thing Hogan was guilty of was being

a nice guy and a surprisingly good dancer. Still, Rachel felt bad about how she had left things with Zach. Maybe she should swing by and say hi—just to patch things up?

"Having a good time?" Hogan asked as he sidled up next to her. He had to raise his voice to be heard over the boisterous honky-tonk music. His accent seemed to get thicker on purpose. "I'm sure this isn't as exciting as wrasslin' gators, but . . ."

Rachel laughed and realized she couldn't think of another thing to say.

Thankfully, the song ended and the first dance began. Hogan guided Rachel toward the center of the dance floor as they moved along with the music. Rachel noticed Tricia dancing nearby. She seemed to be watching them carefully—almost too carefully. For a moment, Rachel worried that Tricia had a crush on Hogan and that she was getting in the middle.

But just then the dance floor slid out from beneath her feet, and Rachel tumbled backward as the swimming pool opened up beneath it.

SPLASH!

As she plunged into the overchlorinated water, she

instantly grasped what was happening. Somebody must have accidentally triggered the floor controls, exposing the swimming pool under the gym floor.

But that wasn't the worst part.

"Help!" Rachel cried out in alarm. "I can't swim!"

She was a cowgirl, not a surfer chick, and with all her other activities, she'd just never bothered to learn how to swim.

"Help me!" she shrieked, on the verge of panic. "Somebody!" A few other kids fell in, but they all swam easily to safety. She was the only one flailing about. She was the only one screaming for help.

"Hang on, Rachel!" Zach shouted. "I'm coming for you!"

But before he could dive in to the rescue, Tricia shoved past him and hurled the business end of a lasso toward Rachel, who grabbed onto it for dear life.

"Hang on, Rachel. Don't let go!" Tricia yelled down as she pulled Rachel in to safety.

"Not a chance," Rachel sputtered, coughing up water. It stung to be saved by Tricia, of all people, but sinkers couldn't be choosers. She clung to the lasso as Hogan

came over and helped Tricia pull her to safety.

But how had this happened, anyway?

Zach watched in dismay as Hogan helped Tricia pull Rachel out of the pool. The floor had stopped retracting. Somebody must have managed to get to the controls. Rachel looked like a drowned rat as she clambered up onto the gym floor, hacking and coughing up water. Her hair and dress were soaked through, and she was shivering like a leaf, from the cold or the shock or both. All around the gym, people stopped to gawk at her. Zach started forward to help her, but Hogan beat him to it.

"Here," Hogan said. "Take my jacket."

He draped his snakeskin jacket over Rachel's trembling shoulders.

"Afraid of the water, are we?" Tricia smirked. "Good thing I could lend a helping hand."

Mortified, Rachel looked like she wanted to turn invisible herself. Her teeth chattered as she mumbled weakly, "I just never got the hang of swimming, that's all."

Personally, Zach didn't think that was such a big deal, but he knew that everybody else in school expected

Rachel to be fearless. Having to be rescued by Tricia didn't look good.

Principal Riggs barged over to check on things. "Somebody get the pool closed . . . pronto!" He looked Rachel over with concern. "Are you all right, Miss Holm?"

"I'm okay," Rachel said, nodding. "Just a little cold and wet. . . ."

"Thanks to Miss Stands here," Riggs congratulated Tricia. "I was impressed by your quick thinking and resourcefulness. You kept your cool in a crisis and may have even saved your classmate from drowning. A commendable job."

"Well, it was the least I could do," Tricia said, "for poor, helpless Rachel."

Applause broke out, with Hogan clapping first and loudest. Pretty soon, the entire gym was cheering for the new hero of the hour: Tricia Stands.

"No, no," Tricia said, feigning modesty. "Rachel was in way over her head. Who am I to say that I'm the real hero?"

"That was it!" Zach realized. "That's what they were

planning all along. Rachel's rep for being the bravest and coolest girl in school gets torpedoed, and Tricia looks like a hero." Zach shook his head in disgust. "She's going to be elected class president for sure."

"But what can we do about it now?" Aaron asked. "We figured it out too late. Tricia and Hogan have already won. We can't turn back time."

Zach smiled as a crazy idea occurred to him. He clapped Aaron on the back. "Or maybe we can."

"Maybe we can what?" Aaron asked.

"Turn back time."

CHAPTER 8

"Darn it," Mr. King said. "I burned the toast again."

It was the morning after the dance, and the Kings were having breakfast at home. Zach and Sophie and their parents milled about the kitchen. The smell of charred bread polluted the atmosphere, threatening to set off the smoke detector on the ceiling.

"I keep telling you we need to get a new toaster," Mrs. King said. "But in the meantime, maybe you can unburn it?"

"Certainly." Mr. King put the blackened bread back

into the toaster and fiddled with his old-fashioned wrist watch, an antique bronze timepiece with a nearly faded engraving of an eagle at its center. His fingers gripped a tiny dial on the watch. "Let's just turn back the clock a few moments."

Zach watched as his father used the magic watch to reverse time and undo the last few minutes. A familiar sensation like static electricity gave Zach goose bumps as time flowed backward and the toast "unburned."

"There, that should do it." Mr. King plucked two lightly browned slices of bread from the toaster. They smelled like toast this time, not charcoal. "If at first, you don't succeed . . ."

Try, try again, Zach thought.

He eyed his dad's watch. In theory, only his dad could use its magic, but that was what Zach had thought about Sophie's glasses as well. If he could borrow Sophie's powers, maybe he could use his dad's watch, too?

Which would give me a chance to rewind to last night's dance, Zach thought, *and save Rachel from having the worst night of her life!*

Zach was excited by his plan but tried not to show it.

He knew better than to ask his dad for a do-over on the dance. Mr. King felt strongly that using his watch too freely kept people from learning from their mistakes. He'd also said more than once that turning back time can have all sorts of unintended consequences if not done with the proper care. Unburning a couple of pieces of toast by turning the clock back a few minutes was one thing, but Zach knew that his dad would never let him rewind things all the way back to last night's dance.

Too bad that's exactly what I have to do, Zach thought.

He hadn't figured out Tricia and Hogan's plan in time to save Rachel last night, but if he had a second chance, he was sure he could set things right. He just had to get his hands on his dad's watch.

Or maybe a copy of the watch?

I'm going to need some help here, he realized. *Good thing I have plenty of cousins!*

And one sneaky little sister.

"Okay, we have to move fast," Zach said several hours later, "before Dad notices that his watch is missing."

Zach sat in front of his laptop, while Sophie looked over

his shoulder. He had his bedroom door closed, but he could still hear his dad taking a shower in the bathroom down the hall. The only time Mr. King ever took off the watch was when he took his evening shower, so Sophie had seized this opportunity to turn invisible and snatch the watch from the nightstand in their parents' bedroom. Then she'd just have to put it back where it belonged before their dad was done showering.

"We're ready when you are," his cousin Andy said from the left half of the laptop's screen. He was wearing his trademark silver sunglasses. His own room, many miles away, could be glimpsed behind him.

"Right," Cousin Gwen said from a separate window on the right side of the screen. The split-screen effect made it look like they were sitting right next to each other even though they were actually in two different locations. Her once-blue cotton-candy hair was dyed purple now. "Let's get this show on the road."

It had taken Zach most of the day to set things up with his cousins, and to wait for his dad to take off his watch, but everything was in place now.

"Thanks, guys," Zach said. "I really appreciate this."

"No problem," Andy replied. "But do you really think you can make my magic object work for you?"

Good question, Zach thought. "That's what we're going to find out."

He put on Andy's sunglasses, which he had never done before. Was it just his imagination, or did he feel a peculiar tingle behind his eyes as he looked through the shades? He held the borrowed wristwatch up in front of his eyes so that it was reflected in the mirrored lenses.

"Center the reflections and concentrate," Andy coached him. "You really need to focus your magic to make it work. It took me a while to get the hang of it."

"That's what I keep telling him," Sophie said. "Practice makes perfect."

But Zach didn't have time for lots of trial and error. He needed a copy of the watch right away. Peering at the watch through the lenses, he tapped the bridge of the glasses frames just like he'd seen Andy do many times before.

Presto, change-o . . . copy!

At first, nothing happened. Zach started to worry that

the incident with Sophie's glasses had been just a freak, one-time thing. Like with the ice cubes or the vending machine.

"Keep concentrating," Gwen encouraged him. "You can do it."

"Maybe if you start slow," Andy suggested, "and use just one eye?"

Taking his advice, Zach shut his right eye and stared as hard as he could through the left one, which started to water from the effort. The tingle turned into a strange, painless sort of throbbing sensation, like the magic was building up inside his eyeball. He tapped the frames again and, all at once, a miniature reflection of the watch popped out of the left lens and magically embiggened to full size. Zach caught the new watch before it hit the ground and put it down on the desk next to the real one. The two watches looked totally identical.

"OMG, it worked!" Gwen exclaimed. "You just borrowed Andy's magic!"

"Word!" Andy agreed. He stared in amazement from his half of the screen. "So does this mean you can use *anyone's* magic object?"

"Looks like it."

Zach could barely believe it himself.

"Just be careful, big brother," Sophie pointed out. "We've spent years training. We all know that magic isn't easy to control—even after you've been doing it forever."

Their cousins were impressed anyway.

"You must have some kind of all-purpose magic," Gwen speculated. "It must work with any sort of magic object."

"I guess . . ." Zach shrugged. "To be honest, I'm still trying to figure it out."

"*We're* all trying to figure it out," Sophie added. "But it's a puzzle."

"Which we can crack another time," Zach said, all too aware that his dad wasn't going to stay in the shower forever. They were cutting it close here. "First, I need to help out Rachel, like I was telling you."

He took off Andy's sunglasses and handed them to Gwen, who passed them back to Andy, from one computer window to another. Zach couldn't help but think about how handy it would be to have Gwen's computer powers as well. He was starting to get excited about his newfound abilities when he heard the shower shut off. His dad would be looking for the missing watch any moment now.

"Thanks again," he told his cousins. "Dad's out of the shower. Gotta motor."

"Just remember, that new watch is just a copy, a reflection," Andy said, sliding his shades back on as he got ready to log off. "It's going to fade away. Copies don't last. Remember that."

"Gotcha!" Zach handed the real watch to Sophie, being careful not to mix it up with the copy. "We need to get this back where you found it."

"Piece of cake." Sophie tucked the watch in her pocket and turned invisible. Her voice seemed to come from nowhere. "Be right back."

Zach tucked the duplicate watch in a desk drawer just as he heard his dad stroll out of the hall bathroom, humming to himself.

"Hey, Dad . . . Dad," Zach called out, to buy Sophie a few precious moments. "You got a minute?"

"Sure, Son." Mr. King detoured into Zach's room,

wearing a bathrobe and slippers. "What's up?"

Zach's mind went blank as his imagination failed him. "Um, er, that is . . . what day is it?"

"Saturday, you silly," Sophie interrupted, appearing in the doorway. She flashed Zach an A-OK sign behind their dad's back, signaling that the watch was back where it belonged. "Really, Zach, sometimes I don't know where your head is at."

"Me either," Zach said. "Just lost track of time, I guess."

Sophie rolled her eyes at the "time" joke.

Mr. King scratched his head, looking slightly puzzled by the exchange. "Is that all you needed, Zach?"

"Absolutely," Zach said, thinking of the duplicate watch. "Thanks, Dad!" He was more than ready now.

Operation Do-Over was a go!

CHAPTER 9

"So how does this work again?" Aaron asked.

He and Zach met up behind the school gym. It was Sunday morning, so there was nobody around but them, which was the whole idea. Dew covered a narrow strip of lawn around the perimeter of the gym. Rusty metal Dumpsters were tucked away in the rear of the building, out of sight and out of mind. In short, it was a good spot to avoid being observed while you tried to change history.

The boys were dressed up for a dance that was now

a couple of days in the past, but, according to Zach, it didn't have to stay that way. Aaron was having trouble wrapping his mind around that idea. Time travel was not something he was used to, and thinking about it too much made his head hurt.

"Okay, one more time." Zach pointed to the retro bronze watch on his wrist. "I use this copy of my dad's watch to rewind time back to the night of the dance, then we stop Hogan from dancing Rachel into Tricia's trap, Rachel doesn't fall into the pool, Tricia doesn't get to play hero, Rachel wins the presidency, the AV Club keeps its funding, and everything turns out better . . . for our side."

"Got it," Aaron said, "I think."

He had left Michael at home this time since he wasn't sure if time travel agreed with cats. The last thing they needed right now was for Michael to cough up a hairball in reverse. Aaron got grossed out just thinking about it.

"And nobody else will notice time running backward?"

"Not even my folks will notice," Zach said, "so we can fix Friday night without anyone knowing. And nobody, except you and me, will remember what happened to Rachel." He turned toward the gym. "I really appreciate you coming along with me, by the way. You ready to do this?"

Aaron checked to make sure his camera's battery was fully charged and the drive still had plenty of memory. No way was he not documenting this operation on video. How often did you get a chance to film the past when it was actually happening . . . again?

"Almost," he told Zach. "Just one more thing."

He rescued a small packet of mustard from his jacket pocket and, before Zach could object, squirted a big glob of mustard into Zach's face.

"To boost the magic," he explained. "Maybe."

"Dude!" Zach yelped as he swept the mustard out of his eyes. "You had to go with the spicy. That stuff stings. You really need to stop doing that!"

"Better safe than sorry," Aaron said with a shrug. "I figured best case, it helps your powers. Worst case, you're just delicious!"

"Dude . . . whatever. Okay, you ready?"

"Ready," Aaron said as bravely as he could muster.

"No time like the present," Zach said as Aaron centered him in the view frame, "to rewind to the past."

Zach started turning the dial on the watch backward, causing its hour and minute hands to move counter-clockwise. He felt that familiar tingling sensation, and he knew the magic was working.

To his amazement, the sun arced backward across a clear blue sky, sinking into the east, as Sunday morning rolled back into Saturday night before it rose again in the west as Saturday afternoon returned.

The clock hands gained speed as Zach spun the dial faster and faster, so that hours slipped away like seconds. Saturday afternoon swiftly became Saturday morning. An early bird landed nearby and spit a worm back into the grass. And soon enough it was late Friday night. Cars reversed down a nearby road while a bat flapped backward overhead. A piece of litter flew back inside a passing car. A weed retreated into the pavement.

"Whoa," Aaron said, his eyes wide. "It's like hitting rewind on a TV remote, but it's not TV . . . it's the real world that's backing up!" He swayed unsteadily, looking a little green around the gills. "Is my blood flowing backward in my brain? 'Cause I'm getting dizzy. . . ."

Zach knew how he felt. He was getting jet lag just

standing in one place. Reversing time this fast was more than a little disorienting.

"Hang in there," he said to Aaron. "We're almost there. Just a few hours—I mean *minutes*—more."

"Make it fast," Aaron said. "I think I'm getting time-sick. . . ."

"Don't throw up! You'll ruin your clothes." Zach counted down the remaining time on the watch. "Approaching early Friday evening and . . . we have arrived at our destination!"

He let go of the dial and time stopped going backward a bit more suddenly than he expected. It was like hitting the brakes on your bike way too fast. Zach and Aaron stumbled like they were dizzy before falling and landing with an "oomph" on their butts in the cold, damp grass.

"Ouch," Aaron said, rubbing his hip. "What's with the bumpy landing?"

"Sorry," Zach said as the boys got back on their feet. "My dad makes this look so easy, but I guess he's had a lot of practice. Plus, he doesn't usually go as fast or as far back as we just did."

"No biggie." Aaron patted himself as though to make sure he hadn't left any important parts back in Sunday.

"Could be worse. I don't see any dinosaurs trying to eat us, so I guess we didn't go back *too* far."

"Not even close," Zach said confidently. Bright lights now shone inside the gym. Country-western music, coming from inside the building, confirmed that the dance was happening all over again. "We're right *when* we belong, just in time to save Rachel from being ambushed!"

Zach and Aaron circled the building to the front entrance. The parking lot, which had been completely deserted on Sunday morning, was now packed with cars, and a flood of kids dressed up for the dance poured into the gym.

"Talk about déjà vu," Aaron said. "It's really Friday again—just like you said it would be."

"Welcome back to two days ago," Zach said, grinning. "Let's make it count this time."

"Wait!" Aaron said, looking worried. "We're not going to bump into our earlier selves, are we?"

Zach shook his head. "Doesn't work like that. We didn't actually travel through time. We just rewound the clock, remember?"

They followed the crowd into the gym, which was all

decked out for the dance just the way Zach remembered. The dummy horses were still standing around like they had wandered away from a merry-go-round. A few brave kids were daring to ride the mechanical bull. Scanning the scene, he spotted Hogan showing off his snazzy rope tricks between the refreshments and the dance floor. Rachel was among a big circle of kids watching the show. Zach was relieved to see that everything was exactly the way it had been.

Great, he thought. There was still time to stop Tricia and Hogan. *I just need to steal that dance from Hogan— and if I'm lucky, dump him in the pool.*

"Get your camera ready," Zach told Aaron. "This is going to be good."

Zach had come fully prepared for this mission. Reaching into his vest pocket, he fished out Sophie's magic pink glasses. It had not been easy talking her into lending them to him again, and whether or not he pulled this off, he would owe her big-time.

"You sure this is a good idea?" Aaron asked. "Remember what happened at the mall."

Zach winced at the memory. "That was my first try. I

know what I'm doing now."

"If you say so." Aaron's gaze drifted toward the snack table. A speculative expression came over his face. "Hmm—"

"Forget it." Zach could guess what was going through his friend's brain. "Don't even think about that ranch dressing."

"What about Tabasco sauce?"

"No! We turned back time, and we're just going with the glasses. We're good."

"Okay, okay," Aaron muttered. "For now."

Zach maneuvered over to a quiet corner of the gym, away from the roaming students and chaperones, where he slipped the glasses on and turned invisible. He glanced down to make sure that both his body *and* his clothes had completely disappeared from sight.

"Yikes!" Aaron yelped as Zach vanished before his eyes. He reached for the seemingly empty air. A sweaty hand groped Zach's face. "Zach? Is that you?"

"Who else?" Zach peeled Aaron's fingers away.

"I knew what to expect," Aaron said, "but it's still pretty freaky when somebody disappears right in front of you. It's like you're not really real anymore."

"That's the idea," Zach whispered to Aaron. "Hogan won't see me coming . . . literally."

Aaron nodded and got his camera ready. "Just make it YouTube-friendly."

"Trust me, everyone's going to want to see this again."

Zach wound invisibly through the crowd, taking care not to get in anyone's way, until he reached the circle of kids and teachers watching Hogan's rope tricks. He elbowed his way past Tricia, who yelped in surprise as an unseen force bumped her aside.

"Hey!" she blurted. "Who did that?"

Zach bit down on his lip to keep from laughing. The baffled look on Tricia's face nearly made this whole stunt worthwhile.

Now for Hogan, he thought.

The crowd had cleared a space to give Hogan room to twirl his lasso around. He jumped in and out of a spinning flat loop with both feet. Zach had to admit that his moves were pretty slick—but not for long.

Like a ghost, Zach crept up on Hogan. He planned to grab the lasso and throw it back over Hogan, so that it would look like he'd accidentally roped himself.

Zach glanced back over his shoulder to make sure Aaron was getting this all on video. Then he darted forward and reached for the lasso.

And missed.

Frowning, he tried to snag it again.

And missed.

Invisible fingers caught only empty air. The problem, Zach realized, was that he couldn't see what he was doing. Apparently, hand-eye coordination really suffered when the eye couldn't locate the hand.

No wonder Sophie had warned him that he'd need more practice!

Hogan twirled the lariat behind his back, drawing applause from the spectators, including Rachel and Principal Riggs. Frustrated, Zach lunged for the lasso one more time—and finally caught hold of it.

Then his touch turned the rope invisible, too.

Startled, Hogan let go of the rope, causing Zach to tumble backward. He tried to get control of the unseen lasso, but it whipped around him, tangling up his legs. Zach stumbled through the audience toward the refreshments.

Uh-oh . . .

Zach saw the jumbo-size plastic punchbowl filled to the brim with disaster coming a second before he slammed into the table. Gallons of cold lemonade splashed down on him, drenching him completely. Ice cubes and lemon slices skittered across the dance floor. The bowl rested on Zach's head like a hat, and the impact knocked Sophie's glasses off, causing Zach to turn visible again. Aaron dropped his camera and dived after the glasses before they could be stomped on.

"Watch your step, everyone!" Aaron shouted. "Runaway glasses!"

Sprawled on the gym floor, soaked to the skin, Zach watched as Principal Riggs marched across the floor toward him. Hogan's soggy lasso was still tangled around Zach's legs. Lemonade dripped down his face.

There was no getting out of this tough spot.

"Zach King!" Principal Riggs stomped toward him, red-faced and fuming. "I should have known you'd be behind all this!" He scratched his shiny bald head, obviously trying to make sense of it all. "Let me guess. You were hiding beneath the table . . . in order to pull off another of your ridiculous magic tricks?"

"Um, something like that," Zach said lamely. He couldn't explain what had really happened without giving away his family's long-held secrets. As far as Principal Riggs and the rest of the world was concerned, Zach's "magic" was all just tricks and illusions.

"One more year," Principal Riggs sighed, and turned his gaze upward. "All I wanted was to get through my last year without any trouble. Just one year. And I'd go off, bait my lures, catch some fish, enjoy the quiet breezes in the Gulf of Mexico . . . but then you came along, Zach King." He buried his face in his hands. "What did I ever do to deserve this?"

Zach couldn't help but feel a little sorry for the principal. He'd just wanted make things go right for Rachel this time, not make Principal Riggs cry.

Untangling himself from the wet rope, Zach looked sheepishly at the principal. "Want to talk about fishing instead?"

"What I want," Riggs said, "is to see you in my office—again!—bright and early Monday morning. But in the meantime, you are hereby banished from this

dance and these premises for the rest of the evening, effective immediately." His stern gaze swung toward Aaron. "And that goes for you, too, young man!"

"Me?" Aaron hastily hid the hot-pink glasses behind his back. "What did I do?"

"Don't play innocent with me," Riggs said. "You two are thick as thieves." He pointed toward the exit. "Make tracks, both of you, unless you want Saturday detention—again!"

Zach's heart sank. If he and Aaron were kicked out of the dance, how were they going to keep Rachel from being sabotaged again?

Zach scrambled to his feet, trying to not to slip in the spilled lemonade. He took the punch bowl off his head, and a stray lemon slice fell out of his hair and onto the floor. Peering past Riggs, he saw Rachel standing next to Hogan, looking embarrassed. He tried to make eye contact with her, but she shook her head and looked away.

Zach couldn't blame her. He realized just how bad this must look from her perspective. He opened his mouth to warn her, but what was he supposed to say?

Rachel, don't dance with Hogan? Make sure you're

wearing a life preserver?

He knew just how crazy that would sound, but he needed to say something, to try to warn her.

"Rachel," he began. "Don't dance—"

But Riggs didn't give him a chance to explain. "You heard me, Zach." He took Zach by the arm and led him firmly toward the door, while making sure that Aaron got the message as well. "Get moving."

The last thing Zach saw, before the principal escorted him out the door, was Hogan leading Rachel out onto the dance floor.

After all that, they hadn't changed anything!

"Well, that sucks," Aaron said outside. He handed Sophie's glasses back to Zach for safekeeping. "What are we going to do now?"

A stubborn look came over Zach's face. "There's only one thing we can do."

"What's that?"

Zach looked at his magic watch.

"Try again."

CHAPTER 10

"Wait—another do-over?" Aaron asked. "Are you serious?"

The boys were walking home from the dance through a quiet suburban neighborhood. Neither of them wanted to call their parents for a ride, not after being expelled from the dance by the principal. Zach got his jacket from the coat closet. His soggy clothes hung heavily on him. His socks and shoes squished with every step.

"It's the only way," he said. "All we did this time was make things worse. To undo all that, we *have* to

try it one more time."

Aaron looked doubtful. "Don't you think that might be pushing our luck?"

"Look at it this way," Zach said. "Do you really want to report to the principal's office on Monday?"

"No way!" Aaron shuddered at the thought. "We just got over doing detention for the alligator mess. Riggs is going to throw the book at us for sure."

"And then some," Zach agreed. "And honestly, we'd also be doing Riggs a favor by undoing everything that just happened. He looked like he was practically ready to retire on the spot. We need another do-over . . . for everyone's sake."

"Like restarting a video game after you get killed?"

"Exactly!" Zach thought that was a perfect comparison. "We didn't make it to the end of *Pumpkin Zombies IV: The Final Carving* the first time through, but we beat the final level eventually."

"Yeah, after *seventeen* tries," Aaron pointed out.

Zach glanced nervously at the duplicate watch, all too aware that the magical copy came with an expiration date. Was the bronze casing already looking a little

worn and duller? Zach couldn't tell for sure. He could only hope that it would last long enough for them to get one more do-over dance.

They were getting nearer to Zach's house. He wasn't looking forward to explaining to his parents why he was soaked in lemonade, but if the next do-over fixed things, that wouldn't matter in the long run. His epic fail with the punch bowl would never happen—and nobody but he and Aaron would ever remember it.

"But what exactly are we going to do differently next time?" Aaron asked.

Zach wasn't entirely sure, but he knew one thing for certain.

"No more invisibility. That's just asking for trouble." He resolved to give Sophie her glasses back as soon as he got home. "I'm going to need another kind of magic."

"Like what?" Aaron asked.

"I'm still working on that part," Zach admitted, "so let's take the night, come up with a plan, and then we'll get together tomorrow, same place, same time, and figure that out."

Aaron groaned. "Ugh, I already feel dizzy again."

CHAPTER 11

The next day the boys rewound time again for what would be their third chance at a happy ending to the big dance.

By now, Zach barely noticed the music and decorations at the dance. Been there, done that. He was keeping his eye on the prize.

"You know what they say: third time's the charm," he told Aaron as they worked their way to the dance floor.

"Who says that exactly?" Aaron asked.

Zach wasn't sure. "Um, 'they'?"

"That's what I thought," Aaron said. As ever, he had his camera ready to record the operation for posterity and/or social media. "You sure you know what you're doing?"

"Don't worry." Zach reached into his jacket and took out a very special deck of playing cards. "I've got it— this time."

Thanks to Gwen's computer wizardry and the modern miracle of long-distance video conferencing, Zach had borrowed the magic playing cards from yet another of his many cousins, Kristi, who had dazzled everyone with her amazing card tricks at Great-Grandpa King's birthday party.

Forget invisibility, Zach thought. *This kind of magic I can handle.*

Zach moved across the dance floor, slipping between friends and chaperones, to get to where Hogan and Rachel were *before* Hogan could start showing off his rope tricks. Zach pushed his way through a group of kids who were square dancing energetically just in time to see Hogan lift a lasso from a saddle that was conveniently mounted on one of the stationary horses near where they were.

"Love the decorations," Hogan told Rachel. "Makes me feel right at home." He toyed with the rope for a moment as if he were getting the feel of it. "You know," he said, as though the idea had just occurred to him, "I happen to know a few tricks I could—"

"Tricks?" Zach interrupted, barging in. "Did somebody mention tricks?"

Rachel looked surprised to see him—and a little worried. "Zach?"

"You know me," Zach said to everyone in earshot. "Tricks are my middle name. Check this out!"

He fanned the cards out in his hands like a professional. Magic made it easy. The cards practically moved under their own power. He collapsed the deck with a dramatic flourish, then fanned them out again. This time all fifty-two cards were the king of clubs. He streamed the cards from one hand to another, back and forth, then revealed that they were all now the queen of hearts.

A second later, they were all jokers.

"Uh-oh!" Zach said, hamming it up. "Somebody better call Batman!"

Gasps and applause greeted the magic tricks as Hogan scowled. He was left on the sidelines with nothing but a boring piece of rope to twirl. Even Principal Riggs watched Zach show off his card tricks. Rachel applauded as Zach pulled a card from Principal Riggs's jacket. It was the same card he was holding at the bottom of the deck. Rachel even winked at Zach.

He could tell she was happy for him.

Things were finally going his way. Why try to sabotage Hogan when he could just upstage him instead?

"Keep your eyes on the cards," Zach told the crowd. "You ain't seen nothing yet!"

He collected the cards into the deck, then flung them upward with a flick of his wrist. The cards shot into the air like a geyser, streaming all the way to the ceiling. Wide-eyed kids and teachers craned their necks back to watch the cards climb a whole lot higher than a mere fifty-two cards could possibly reach. It was like the cards were multiplying before their eyes.

Which was exactly what they were doing.

Top that, Zach thought. He smirked at Hogan, who was giving Zach some serious stink eye by now. *I'm on to you.*

"Anybody up for a game of fifty-two pickup?"

He held out his hand, expecting the cards to do a U-turn in midair and dive straight back into his palm, just like they had done for Kristi at the birthday party.

But instead the cards started spraying out in all directions while multiplying at a ridiculous rate. An endless flurry of clubs, spades, hearts, and diamonds swarmed the gym, swooping and soaring wildly through the air. The cards zipped through streamers, shredding ribbons, and careened into balloons, popping them on contact. The *ooh*s and *aah*s turned into "Yikes!" and "Run for your life!" as people ducked for cover. Even the Buckeye Barn Razors stopped playing as the cards swarmed their instruments like bees. The banjo player got so freaked out, he swung his instrument at the swarm and accidentally whacked the fiddler in the head. Zach heard a loud *twang* over the screaming and shouting and thought, "Oh, that can't be good."

"Zach!" Rachel screamed, batting a jack of diamonds away from her face. "Do something! Get these crazy cards of yours under control!"

"I'm trying!"

He ran after the cards, waving his arms to try to get their attention.

"Come back here!" he called out. "Get back in the deck!"

Pandemonium broke out. Frantic students, freaked out by the storm of cards, knocked into the dummy horses and ducked behind bales of hay. Aaron was madly trying to get it all on video, but even he had to jump backward to avoid to getting seriously paper-cut by an ace of spades. He slipped on a burst balloon, stumbled to keep his balance—and fell over into the punch bowl.

Splash!

No, Zach thought. *Not again!*

Aaron was drenched in lemonade. History was basically repeating itself—but with a vengeance. Zach could already see where this was going, and it wasn't good.

But first he had to get the runaway cards in line.

"Shuffle!" he shouted at them. "Reshuffle!"

That did the trick. The cards joined up like a flock of geese high above Zach's head before flopping to the ground in front of him. Zach gathered them up and jammed them back into his pocket.

He sighed in relief.

"Zach King!" Principal Riggs cried out in exasperation. "I should have known that—"

Zach had seen this episode before. He didn't need to catch the rerun.

"I know, I know," he said glumly. "Your office, Monday. Out the door now, effective immediately."

"Er, that's right." Riggs was briefly thrown for a loop. "You took the words right out my mouth." He looked over at Aaron, who was soaked with lemonade. "And as for you, young man . . ."

"Don't play innocent, thick as thieves, yada yada," Aaron said, skipping ahead. "We know the drill."

As Zach marched out of the gym, he noticed that things were starting to calm down now that the cards were not zipping about everywhere. For a moment, he dared to hope that maybe the whole dance would be called off, which would at least save Rachel from the social catastrophe awaiting her.

"Sorry if we ruined the dance," Zach said as they reached the exit doors.

"Don't be absurd," Riggs said. "I'm not going to let

your juvenile practical jokes spoil everyone's good time."
He nodded at the Barn Razors, who hesitantly started playing again. "You see, the show must go on."

Zach saw Hogan taking Rachel's hand.

"That's what I was afraid of," he said.

He had failed again, even worse than before, which meant only one thing.

He had to do it all again!

CHAPTER 12

The gym had an elevated running track overlooking the main floor. It was off-limits during the dance, but Zach had crept up there without too much difficulty. He perched on the track, spying on the dance below. Cardboard wings, borrowed from his cousin Steve, were strapped to his arms. The wings were rectangular pieces of plain brown cardboard that had once belonged to a refrigerator box. Zach could already feel the magic pulsing. The wings were struggling to flap, lifting him up off his toes, eager to take flight.

He was ready for liftoff.

Please let things work out this time, he thought.

Zach was nervous about attempting another do-over after his last two epic fails, but what else could he do? Even after the playing cards went berserk, Rachel *still* ended up in the pool.

I have to get things right, Zach thought.

He peered down from the track, scoping out the scene. Hogan and Rachel were already on the dance floor, kicking up their heels to a lively country-western tune. Zach's latest plan was to swoop in right before the first dance. This way he could make sure that Rachel didn't get anywhere near Tricia's trap. If he pulled this off, it would be even more spectacular than that drone idea Hogan had stolen before.

If he could pull it off. . . .

Aaron was already waiting below to catch the whole thing on video. Zach tensed up as he heard the bouncy honky-tonk song winding up. By now, he knew the Barn Razors' playlist by heart. The dance was coming up next.

"Here goes nothing," he murmured. "Up, up, and away."

The worst part, Zach realized, was that this dance had been more of a disaster than the last one!

His cousin's wings were trashed, and he noticed the duplicate watch was looking the worse for wear. He didn't have much time left to set things right.

I need to do a do-over, he realized. *Now, more than ever.*

CHAPTER 13

Zach and Aaron huddled behind the gym after Principal Riggs had thrown them out of the dance. They could hear the music and laughter start up again. But Zach could also tell that the copy of his dad's watch was about to give up the ghost. Bits of corroded bronze were flaking off it, then vanishing like sparks drifting away from a campfire. It was on the verge of evaporating completely.

"No time to regroup," he told Aaron, showing him the timepiece. "We have to go back now, even farther than before."

"How far?" Aaron asked.

"A couple of days at least, to buy us enough time to hatch a one-hundred-percent disaster-proof plan . . . if the watch can hold it together just a little bit longer."

"I'm not sure my stomach can handle it," Aaron said, burping. "I ate a lot of dip at the dance." But Zach wasn't really worried about his friend's indigestion. He had to stop Hogan and Tricia the only way he knew how. He spun the dial and stared in amazement as time started scrolling backward again.

Cars reversed up to the school and kids dressed for the dance jumped backward into their seats. Zach kept spinning the dial, wanting to go back to Wednesday at least, but then his copy of his dad's watch dissolved into nothingness before his eyes. For a moment, it seemed like he could still *feel* it around his wrist, like a phantom bracelet, but then even the sensation faded away. There was nothing around his wrist but air.

Time stopped rewinding. To Zach's dismay, the watch's last gasp had only managed to get them back to earlier that same evening. They barely had any time at all to fix things—and this was their last chance.

"That's it," he told Aaron. "No more watch. No more do-overs. This time everything counts."

"It's on," Aaron said. "It's on like Donkey Kong!"

The boys found a back door that was cracked open and snuck into the upper level. They peered down as volunteers finished getting all the decorations and stuff in place, converting the gym into a makeshift ranch. The mechanical bull was set up, along with the haystacks and mock horses. Helium balloons were filled and released to float up to the ceiling. The Barn Razors were warming up. Somebody filled the punch bowl with lemonade.

"Any idea what we're going to do this time?" Aaron asked. "'Cause, you know, our track record isn't all that great so far."

"Those were just practice runs," Zach decided. "This, my friend . . . this is the real deal."

He started to peek at his wristwatch to see exactly how much time they had before the dance started, only to remember that the magic timepiece was history. Checking out the gym's clock instead, he gulped as he saw that the dance was starting any minute now. Cars were already pulling back into the parking lot, dropping off gangs of kids. Zach had to think fast.

There was no time to work out some kind of magic-object exchange with his cousins. He was going to have to make do with whatever he could get quickly.

He pulled out his phone and dialed the person he trusted the most in the world.

"Hello? Sophie? You're not going to like this, but I need a *huge* favor! Yes, another one . . ."

CHAPTER 14

Time was running out . . . for the last time.

Zach fidgeted beside Aaron as the gym filled with kids and the dance got underway. He waited anxiously for Sophie to show up while things played out just as they always had. Hogan showed off his rope tricks again. He and Rachel hit the dance floor again. The Barn Razors broke out a countrified version of the classic party song "Shout." The fateful dance was coming up again. . . .

"I'm really getting tired of hearing the same old songs again and again," Aaron said. "It's as if the shuffle function on my phone is permanently broken."

"Don't worry," Zach said. "After tonight, you'll never have to hear the Barn Razors again." He peered through the crowd, searching for his occasionally invisible little sister, who really should have been here by now. Everything was depending on her being on time. "What's keeping Sophie?"

"Chill, dude," Aaron said. "She'll get here."

"I hope so—otherwise all this was for nothing."

Zach kept a close watch on Hogan and Rachel. She was dancing like she didn't have a care in the world. Gosh, she was pretty! It killed Zach that she had no idea what was in store for her only a few minutes from now.

"C'mon, Sophie," Zach whispered, hoping that maybe she had shown up invisibly for some reason. His hands searched the empty air around him. "Paging Sophie?"

But nobody answered. The air was just air.

"If she doesn't show up soon," Zach said, "I'm going to have to do something . . . magic or no magic. I can't let Hogan and Tricia prank Rachel like this."

"What are you thinking?" Aaron asked.

"I don't know. Maybe barge onto the dance floor and

call out Hogan. Granted, I don't have any evidence. I'd make a total fool of myself. But at least I'd stop them, right?"

"Dude!" Aaron blurted. "That's not going to go over well with Principal Riggs . . . and if Rachel thinks that you're just trying to ruin her good time, which she will, she'll never speak to you again!"

"Yeah, but—"

"Dude, just hang tight," Aaron said as the last number started winding up. "Sophie will get here. I know she will."

"I can't wait any longer, dude. I have to do something."

Heart pounding, Zach headed toward the dance floor, determined to break up Hogan and Rachel's dance one way or another. Then a voice called out to him from behind.

"Hey, bro!" Sophie said. "Forgetting something?"

Zach spun around to find his sister directly behind him, holding out their mom's magic ring.

"Don't ask me what it took to get this," she said. "You owe me big-time . . . yet again."

Without thinking, Zach gave Sophie a huge hug. His heart leaped. He snatched the ring from her hand.

"Thanks, sis!"

His mom's ring was possibly the most versatile magic object in the King family. Transmuting one object to another could be used in a million different creative ways. The only limit, as far as Zach knew, was its user's imagination. Zach wasn't going to try anything too complicated this time. His last-ditch plan was to use his mother's ring to turn all the water in the pool into a trampoline so that Rachel would bounce up safely after she fell. No one would have to know that she couldn't swim, her fearless image wouldn't take a hit, and, most important, Tricia wouldn't get a chance to play hero. He just needed to wait for Hogan to set the trap, then rush over and work his magic at the perfect right time. *Easy-peasy,* he thought, *now that I've got this ring.*

Zach slipped the ring on his finger. He was expecting a slight tingle. What he got was a sudden jolt of energy that shot up his arm and practically made his hair stand on end. Zach felt like he was holding on to a live electrical cable. It was hard to believe that his mom just walked around wearing it like it was no big deal. She made it look so easy.

"Wow," he said, shaking off the shock. "I had no idea. . . ."

"Oh, yeah, Mom's the real deal," Sophie said. "I hope I don't need to remind you of what happened last time."

"I get it this time—really." Zach cut her off before she could really get rolling with her lecture. "But we're talking desperate times here."

"Just be careful," Sophie called after him as Zach turned to make his way through the crowd over to Rachel.

But Zach had underestimated how tricky it would be to cross the packed dance floor. Dancing couples didn't notice him and didn't give way, so Zach had to work his way around the fringe of the dance floor as Hogan led Rachel toward the center of the floor—and disaster.

"Oh, crud," Zach said. "Hurry, hurry, hurry. . . ."

He was in such a rush that he wasn't really looking where he was going, and he accidentally walked smack into one of the papier-mâché horses.

"Ouch!"

Dazed, he looked around for Rachel and Hogan, only to realize that he had completely lost sight of them. For all he knew, he was way on the wrong side of the dance floor with half his class blocking his view. Frantic, he scrambled up onto the dummy horse to see over the crowd. He grabbed the reins to keep from sliding off it.

If only this was a real horse, he thought, *I could ride to the rescue. . . .*

It was just a random thought, but the magic ring didn't know that. The ring activated in a big way, creating a blinding flash that briefly lit up the entire gym, and the horse beneath Zach suddenly came to life.

And so did all the other dummy horses in the gym.

As well as the mechanical bull.

"Wait!" Zach shouted at the ring. "I didn't mean it!"

Just like in an old cartoon, one by one the horses ran straight into the painted barn door—and vanished into the scenery. Horace, displaying more energy and enthusiasm than Zach had ever thought the sleepy bulldog was capable of, expertly herded the wild horses toward the barn until all that was left was one lone straggler and the horse Zach was sitting on. Energy coursed through the magic ring on Zach's finger, keeping the painted door open just a little while longer.

How about that? Zach thought. *I think I'm finally getting the hang of this.*

It was amazing what you could do as long as you kept calm and didn't lose control of the magic. And it definitely helped if you were trying to do the right thing.

Horace caught up with the last frantic pony, who was galloping in circles around the badly scuffed dance floor. An impressively deep bark sent the pony running into the painting with the others.

"Nice work!" Zach praised the dog.

The only real horse left was the one beneath him. Zach slid out of the saddle and onto the floor.

"Thanks for the ride, pal. I couldn't have done it without you."

He swatted the panting horse on the rump and it galloped into the painted barn as well. His work done, Horace slumped down on the floor to take a well-deserved nap. Within moments, he was asleep again and snoring like crazy.

"So much for that stampede," Zach said.

"Ahem." Rachel called his attention to the bull, which was still tied up on the floor. "You're not quite done yet!"

"Right!" Zach said. "I almost forgot!"

He hurried over to her and the bull. The ring flashed again—and a large mechanical bull was now now lying on the floor.

"That's better," Rachel said. She started untying the bull's legs. "So, you want to explain to me what exactly this is all about?"

Fortunately for Zach, Principal Riggs hadn't seen a thing. The punch bowl had landed upside-down on his head and he'd spent the entire stampede trying to wrest it off. But it was the weirdest thing. The bowl just

refused to budge. It was almost as though somebody was pressing it down on his head. Somebody who giggled like a little girl.

"This isn't funny!" His voice echoed inside the plastic punch bowl. "If you're holding this bowl on my head, you'll have detention for the rest of your life—and then some!"

He could hear animals galloping around. The clamor of pounding hooves competed with loud neighs and whinnies as he tried to make sense of what was happening. But he couldn't see a thing that was going on.

And then suddenly the hoofbeats got quieter and then quieter still, until the gym was pretty much silent. Riggs was more confused than relieved. If only he could see what was happening. . . .

And then, without warning, the punch bowl lifted up on its own and then toppled over to one side. Principal Riggs thought he heard footsteps running away, but there was nothing in sight except a huge mess. The decorations were splayed everywhere. The mechanical bull had fallen over feet up. The balloons and streamers were destroyed, and the refreshments table had been toppled. And there were no horses at all, not even the papier-mâché ones.

The only kids still left in the gym were Zach, Aaron, and Rachel.

"Wha—what happened?" Riggs stammered. "There was a blinding light, then horses everywhere. . . . I could have sworn I heard horses. . . ."

"Real horses?" Rachel asked, as though she didn't understand the question. She was calmly fiddling with a lasso over by the toppled bull ride. "Now that's weird," she said with a shrug.

Principal Riggs ran his hand over his scalp, trying to figure it out. None of this made any sense.

"But . . . ?"

"Mr. R?" Hogan cautiously snuck out of the locker rooms, where he had run to hide. He was splattered with dung and he smelled like it. "You're not going to let them get away with this, are you?"

The principal scowled. His nose wrinkled in disgust. "Aha—it was you! You're behind all the horses and noise. It has to be. You stink like a stable." The principal dripped lemonade onto the floor. "I misjudged you, Hogan. You're a disgrace to Australia . . . and to this school."

Hogan's face crashed. He tried to wheedle his way back into the principal's good graces. "Say, did I mention some new fly-fishing techniques I've been meaning to show you?"

"That's enough." Riggs held up a palm to silence him. "Get out of my sight . . . and away from my nose!"

Tricia peeked out from behind the overturned bandstand. It looked like the coast was clear, so she decided it was time to cut her losses and call it a night. Getting back at Rachel and Zach would have to wait. She'd had enough of this stupid hoedown.

Too bad we never got to dunk Rachel in the pool, she thought. *After all that planning and preparation.*

It dawned on her that she had somehow lost her new cowboy hat in the commotion. She glanced around the gym, searching for it.

"Looking for something?" Aaron asked.

He held out her hat, which had miraculously survived the stampede. "Thanks for nothing, loser!" Tricia snarled as she snatched it from his pudgy fingers. She plopped it back down onto her silken blond hair. "Don't think you and your freaky friends—"

But she stopped midsentence as something cold and gooey spilled from the hat, down her head, and over her shoulders.

"Smile for the camera," Aaron said. "Say 'ranch dressing'!"

CHAPTER 15

"When do you think they'll announce the winner of the election?" Rachel asked.

"Should be any time now," Zach guessed.

"And I'm ready to capture the results live," Aaron said, patting his camera.

It was the Monday after the dance. The trio was sharing a table in the school cafeteria while they waited anxiously to find out who their next class president was going to be. The dish of the day was microwaved pineapple pizza, which didn't require ketchup, mustard, mayonnaise, or any other condiments, but Zach kept one eye on Aaron anyway. His friend seemed to have finally dropped his crazy ketchup theory, but you never could tell.

"The suspense is killing me," Rachel said.

"Nothing to worry about," Aaron reassured Rachel. "You've got it in the bag now that the whole school's seen you rescue Tricia from that rampaging 'mechanical' bull."

Zach had to agree with Aaron. The video of Rachel roping the bull had gone viral since Aaron had posted it online—as had the footage of Hogan hightailing it out of the gym, thoughtlessly shoving aside anyone in his way instead of helping out with his mad cowboy skills. The part where Hogan took a header into the big, steaming pile of horse manure had already inspired plenty of hilarious GIFs and memes. Last time Zach had checked, the clip had been shared all the way from here to Australia.

"Couldn't happen to a nicer guy," Zach said sarcastically. "That's what I call karma in action."

He glanced at Hogan and Tricia, who had staked out a table on the opposite side of the cafeteria, as far as they could possibly get from Zach and his friends. The two bullies weren't even pretending not to be on the same side anymore. Hogan gave them a dirty look that was a lot less attractive than his fake smiles.

"He had me fooled," Rachel admitted. "I should have believed you when you tried to warn me, Zach."

"And I'm sorry I didn't ask you to the dance first," Zach said. "It just made everything more complicated."

She punched him playfully in the shoulder. "Well, next time don't wait so long."

"I'll keep that in mind," Zach promised.

"*That is*, if Principal Riggs ever works up the nerve to schedule another school dance," Aaron said. Bored, he checked out the news on his phone. "You guys heard the latest story regarding what went on at the dance? Riggs is now blaming it all on a panic set off by a malfunctioning mechanical bull."

"Seriously?" Zach said. "What about the wild horses and everything?"

"Exaggerations, overexcited imaginations, mass hysteria." Aaron counted off the so-called explanations on his fingers. "Everything but magic."

"You think Riggs really believes that?" Rachel asked.

Zach thought it over.

"I think he really *wants* to believe it."

That was good enough for Zach, who was just relieved that the magical stampede wasn't national news. He wasn't too surprised by this, however. One of the big reasons his family's magic had stayed secret for so long was that most of the world would seize on any sort of "rational" explanation, no matter how ridiculous, before admitting that magic was real.

Which was probably why Tricia was keeping her mouth shut, too. She'd just sound like a complete nutcase if she tried telling the truth about Zach.

Works for me, Zach thought.

Tricia scowled as she caught Zach looking her way.

"What are you looking at, freak? One of these days—"

A squawk from the school's public-address system interrupted her. The cafeteria quieted down as Principal Riggs's voice came over the intercom:

"Attention, students and faculty. As principal, I'm pleased to announce that the winner of the sixth-grade class election is . . ."

Rachel sat up straight. Zach held his breath as the principal paused to draw out the suspense.

"Horace, our beloved school mascot."

Cheers and laughter erupted in the cafeteria. Horace, who had been snuffling around the cafeteria looking for leftovers, briefly lifted his head, then went back to chowing down on a dropped pizza crust.

"Seriously?" Rachel said, shaking her head. "I lost to a dog?"

"I know!" Aaron said. "He's not nearly as cute as my cat!"

"Could be worse," Zach pointed out, nodding at Tricia, who got up and stormed out of the room with a furious look on her face. Talk about a sore loser! Hogan stomped off behind her. Zach hoped he would keep on walking until he was back in Australia.

"Good point," Rachel said, chuckling. Unlike Tricia, she could see the funny side of the election results. "I suppose I should go congratulate Horace on his victory."

Zach handed her what was left of his pizza slice. "Don't forget a treat."

"Hang on!" Aaron said. "I want to get this on video!"

"See?" Rachel said. "What would I do without you guys?"

Zach couldn't stop grinning as he and Rachel and Aaron high-fived each other. It seemed that all those do-overs had paid off after all. Maybe Rachel hadn't won the election, but she, Zach, and Aaron were truly a team again. Their friendship was stronger than ever.

That was the biggest victory of all.

"We'll be back soon," Mrs. King said, smiling. "You kids stay out of trouble."

Zach's parents were going to dinner for their weekly date night. Grandpa King had already settled onto the living room couch to babysit. Mr. King checked his wristwatch as they lingered in the front hall of the King house. "We'd better get going. We don't want to miss our reservation."

"Says the man with the magic watch," Mrs. King teased him. Her ring sparkled on her finger, back where it belonged. Sophie had returned the ring to her mother after the dance, apologizing for having "borrowed" it without permission. Her parents had scolded her but had not gotten too upset since there'd been no harm done. Thankfully, neither their mom nor their dad had figured out *why* exactly Sophie had taken the ring, so Zach hadn't had to explain to them about his borrowed magic. He appreciated Sophie taking the fall for him so he could keep attending public school like a "normal" kid.

Mrs. King waved good-bye to her children. "See you later, kids, and don't forget to do your homework."

"Will do, Mom," Zach said. "Have a good time."

"And don't worry," Sophie said, looking over her shoulder at Grandpa, who was already snoring. "I'll keep an eye on Zach while Grandpa sleeps."

"Um, I think you have that backward, sis. I'm keeping an eye on you."

"Yeah, you keep telling yourself that, big brother."

After their parents left the house and the car pulled out of the driveway, Zach and Sophie settled down in the family room to do some gaming. (Homework could wait.) But before Zach could fire up *Jedi Kittens: The Fur Awakens*, Sophie got in front of the TV and looked him in the eye.

"I'm calling in my favors," she said seriously. "You still owe me, remember? For lending you my glasses . . . and getting you Mom's ring?"

"I remember." Zach appreciated her going out on a limb for him when things got rocky. "What do you want?"

"No more borrowed magic. You need to find your own magic, Zach."

"But . . ."

"No buts," she insisted. "You lucked out this time, but messing around with other people's magic objects is just asking for trouble. You need to knock it off . . . or I'll spill the beans to Mom and Dad."

Zach sighed. "You can skip the blackmail. To be honest, I've kinda been thinking the same thing." He remembered how many disasters he'd had to do over before finally getting it right. "Borrowed magic is more trouble than it's worth!"

Sophie nodded.

"Just be patient, big brother. We both know magic isn't done with you yet. You're special somehow . . .

or maybe just a total weirdo."

"Same difference," Zach said.

"You said it, not me."

She sat down on the couch and picked up a game controller.

"So, now that *that's* settled, let's get our gaming on. You want the Dark or the Light Side of the Fur?"

TO BE CONTINUED. . . .

A special thank-you to
Rachel King, David Linker, Aaron Benitez, and Bradley Grimm.

ABOUT THE AUTHOR

Zach King is a twenty-seven-year-old filmmaker who creates videos with a hint of "magic." With more than 25 million followers across his various social platforms, he is one of the hottest names in digital media. He's been featured on *Ellen* and on the red carpet at the Academy Awards—and he's partnered with Lego, Disney, and Kellogg's to create mind-blowing videos. In 2016, Zach and his wife competed in *The Amazing Race* along with other social media superstars. Born and raised in Portland, Oregon, Zach is the author of *Zach King: My Magical Life*. He lives with his family in Los Angeles.

Fill your world
with colour

**Fun-filled adventures
with Puffin Books**

Ready for another story?

Great! Puffin has plenty to share.

Discover them all at **puffin.co.uk** along with:

· Ideas for magical read-along moments

· Playtime printables to keep boredom at bay

· Competitions to win books, toys
and trips away!

puffin.co.uk